SECRET AGENT MUMMY

STEVE COLE

Illustrated by Donough O'Malley

RED FOX

SECRET AGENT MUMMY
A RED FOX BOOK 978 1 849 41818 8

First published in Great Britain by Red Fox
an imprint of Random House Children's Publisher's UK
A Random House Group Company

This edition published 2014

1 3 5 7 9 10 8 6 4 2

Text copyright © Steve Cole, 2014
Logo artwork copyright © Andy Parker, 2014
Cover artwork copyright © Dave Shelton
Interior illustrations copyright © Donough O'Malley, 2014
Ancient Egypt Advisor – Louise Ellis-Barrett

The Random House Group Limited supports the Forest Stewardship Council® (FSC®), the leading international forest-certification organisation. Our books carrying the FSC label are printed on FSC®-certified paper. FSC is the only forest-certification scheme supported by the leading environmental organisations, including Greenpeace. Our paper procurement policy can be found at www.randomhouse.co.uk/environment

MIX
Paper from
responsible sources
FSC® C016897

Set in Bembo MT Schoolbook

Random House Children's Publishers UK,
61–63 Uxbridge Road, London W5 5SA

www.**stevecolebooks**.co.uk
www.**randomhousechildrens**.co.uk
www.**totallyrandombooks**.co.uk
www.**randomhouse**.co.uk

Addresses for companies within The Random House Group Limited can be found at:
www.randomhouse.co.uk/offices.htm

THE RANDOM HOUSE GROUP Limited Reg. No. 954009

A CIP catalogue record for this book is available from the British Library.

Printed and bound in Great Britain by CPI Group (UK) Ltd, Croydon, CR0 4YY

For Tobey and Amy

Chapter One

A Whiff of Weirdness

The house on the hill was so spooky, even ghosts would think twice about visiting after dark. It was big and old. Its jagged roof looked like teeth biting the sky.

Niall Rivers had never come here before,

and hoped he never would again. His mum had been driving around the neighbourhood collecting bric-a-brac for the school fête on Sunday, and the owner of this house had about a hundred tons of junk to give away.

While Mum sorted through billions of boxes in the dark, dusty hall, and the owner stood around watching and smiling, Niall's nostrils quivered from the pong of the place. It smelled like the monkey house at the zoo, with a bit of backed-up toilet thrown in for luck.

"Uh, I think I'll wait outside," Niall murmured.

"Very wise," said the owner from a shadowy corner of the hall, his voice hoarse with age. "There's quite a view. You might be surprised by what you can see."

Niall didn't answer, but made his way outside and took some deep breaths. "Maybe I'll spot a couple of orang-utans using the bathroom. That would explain the niff!" He smiled to himself and glanced up at a dirty window.

For a moment he thought he saw red eyes glaring back at him, but they were gone in a blink.

What was up there? Frowning, Niall went to get a better look.

As he did so, he saw a man duck out of sight behind a tree a short way down the hill. *Looks a bit shifty*, he thought. Unfortunately for the man, the tree was so thin it could hardly hide a squirrel, let alone a human being. Niall could see the man's grey raincoat flapping, and the wide brim of his hat sticking out on either side of the trunk.

"Ah. Um ... Hello, there." The man stuck his head out from behind the tree and smiled at Niall. His eyes were hidden by a pair of dark glasses.

"I am just giving this tree its annual checkup." The man spoke carefully, as if English were not his first language. "You know, checking it for ... um, leaves."

Weirdo, thought Niall.

"Er, right. Well, the owner is just in the house here. Shall I—?"

"No!" said the weirdo quickly. "I have to go. I

have got a whole lot of other trees to inspect." He pulled out a notebook, looked at the house, scribbled something down, and hurried away – straight into another tree. "*Ooof!* Er . . . yes. Like this one. 'Hard trunk'," he noted. Then, with a quick wave at Niall, he staggered off down the driveway.

Niall shrugged and turned back to the house, just as the front door burst open. Mum appeared, struggling with a couple of large cardboard boxes.

"Niall, quick, open the car boot," she gasped. "These weigh a ton."

He did as she asked, but as Mum tried to

squash the boxes in, something fell to the ground. It was a strange-looking model, carved from wood.

"What's that?" Niall stooped to pick up the little wooden figure. It had the body of a man, and the head of a baboon or something. *I knew that house smelled like monkeys*, he thought . . .

But as Niall's fingers closed around the figure –

ZZZAPPP!

It felt as if a herd of nuclear elephants were

trumpeting behind his eyes. Amazing colours blazed through his brain . . .

Then the feeling faded. Niall stood up, staring dumbly at the figure clutched tightly in his hand.

"Hmm, looks a bit Egyptian." Mum plucked the carving from his fingers – but nothing seemed to happen to her. "Might get fifty pence for it."

She chucked it in a box and slammed the boot shut. "Right, that was my last call today. I need to collect Ellie from dance class."

Niall rubbed his tingling eyes. "Uh . . . right."

Mum frowned as she opened the driver's door. "What, no fuss? No moans about having to run around after your little sister? Sure you're OK, Niall?"

"I do feel a bit weird," he admitted as he got into the car. "Maybe the stink in there turned my head funny."

"Shhh!" Mum glanced at the front door, but it had already swung shut. "The owner might be whiffy, but he was very generous. He insisted I take everything."

"Saves him taking it down the dump, I guess."

Niall smiled. "Hey, could we take Ellie down the dump once we've picked her up?"

"That's my son back," Mum sighed, starting the car. "Behave yourself, Niall Rivers . . ."

Niall grinned. "Maybe one day!"

They drove away down the hillside. Niall's head was still spinning when he caught sight of the weirdo in the raincoat behind another tree. He seemed to be peering at the old house through a funny telescope shaped like a long triangle. As the car trundled past, the man ducked down into a bush, then yelped as he realized it was full of thorns.

"Must be a gardener," Mum remarked.

"Or an escaped looper," Niall muttered, as he noted something odd. How could he not have noticed that before?

The looper must have bumped into an awful lot of trees since waving goodbye. His face was *covered* in bandages . . .

Chapter Two

The Pyramid Next Door

That evening passed quickly for Niall. He kept busy making an Ellie-the-Snitch Detector.

Niall loved playing with technology – fiddling with gadgets and inventing new ones. His dumb little sister often tried to spy on him, and Niall was determined to stop her. He sat on his bed trying to connect the motion-sensor from an old toy to the buzzer from an alarm clock. If anyone

 13

came near his bedroom door, the buzzer would warn him. That was the idea, anyway.

After hours of fiddling, Niall felt he was finally getting somewhere, when his door suddenly burst open.

"Hey!" He dived forward to hide his project, and accidentally squashed it with his tum. "Ow!"

"Niall?" The Snitch glared at him suspiciously from the doorway. "What are you up to?"

14

He smiled. "Plotting your doom."

"That's mean," said the Snitch coolly. "I'm telling Mummy."

"What a surprise," said Niall as she trotted away, blonde bunches bouncing. Ellie had made it her mission in life to get him into trouble whenever possible.

"Niall," Mum called wearily a few seconds later, "don't be mean to your sister."

"Fine!" Niall yelled back. He got up, slammed the door shut, and stared crossly at his broken gadget. But his eyes felt hot and prickly. He realized he felt stupidly tired. It was all he could

 15

do to stagger back to his bed and lie down.

Oh, well, I've got the whole school holidays to finish the detector, he thought, dozing off. *Nothing much going on . . . Nothing to worry about . . .*

Those words exploded in Niall's head the moment he woke up the next morning. He pulled open his curtains and saw something completely impossible.

"Huh?" He rubbed sleep from his eyes.

Closed the curtains.

Opened them again.

But the impossible view through his bedroom

window refused to shift.

In the garden next door, there was a pyramid.

A humongous sandstone *pyramid*. As if a crazy lump of Ancient Egypt had dropped out of the sky or pushed up through the ground. Either way . . .

"HUH?!" Niall blinked and rubbed his eyes.

The pyramid refused to budge.

"MUM!" Niall jumped off his bed, sprinted out onto the landing, slid down

the banister, accidentally knocked over the coatstand (and the dozen coats it carried) and crashed into the kitchen.

"Have you seen it?" he panted, "have you seen next door?"

"Seen what?" His mum was eating cereal and reading a magazine. "That house has been empty for months."

"The garden!" Niall grabbed her by the arm. "You're not going to believe it. Come on, look!"

Protesting, his mum allowed herself to be tugged to the window for a bang-on view of the giant pyramid looming over the fence.

She shrugged. "So, the garden's overgrown. Like it was yesterday."

Niall stared at her, baffled. "Don't act like you can't see that pyramid!"

"What pyramid?" Mum shook her head crossly and went back to her cereal. "Niall, it's too early for silly games."

Niall couldn't believe what he was hearing. "But ...!"

Just then, the Snitch came into the kitchen. "Mummy!" she squealed. "Niall knocked over the coatstand again."

Mum sighed and went into the hall to see.

"Shut up, Snitch, and look at this." Niall hauled Ellie by her fluffy pink dressing gown across to the kitchen window. "See? Completely crazy, right?"

Ellie looked at him like he was an alien. "It's a *house*, Niall. There are lots of them around here."

"Stop pretending," he said desperately. "There's a massive pyramid in next door's garden. You've *got* to be able to see it!"

"Mummy," called Ellie, "Niall's gone crazy!"

Mum came back into the kitchen and sat down heavily on her stool. "Guys, please. With your dad away for work, and the fête coming

 21

up, I've got enough to cope with."

Niall stomped back upstairs to his bedroom. *Am I going crazy?* he wondered. The ridiculous pyramid was still there. It even had a triangular chimney perched on its pointy roof.

Mum and the Snitch must be playing some dumb trick on me, thought Niall. *It can't be real . . .*

Can it?

There was only one thing to do – he had to check the pyramid up close. *If it isn't really there, my hand will go straight through the wall and I'll know it's all a trick.*

But what if the pyramid *was* real?

Where had it come from?

Who could be inside?

Niall took a deep breath. There was only one way to find out.

Chapter Three

Something Fishy

Legs trembling, Niall ran down to the bottom of the garden and scrambled over next door's fence. The pyramid before him *looked* solid enough. It had a narrow door and huge triangles for windows. Whatever lay behind them was hidden by dark glass.

Niall marched up to the pyramid before he could chicken out.

As he approached, the door slid slowly open . . .

Run away! yelled a voice in Niall's head.

There's no need, he thought. *I've got to be dreaming.*

No one came out to meet him. As if in a trance, Niall walked into a huge, shadowy hallway. There was no furniture. A fig tree grew out of the sandy floor. Massive Egyptian paintings covered the walls. They showed figures in white skirts and jewellery and strange creatures that were half human, half animal. One had a human body and the head of a baboon . . .

Just like the little statue he'd picked up the day before.

This is getting weirder and weirder, thought Niall.

The door beside him was marked

OPERATIONS ROOM

It slid silently open to reveal a room that *really* blew his mind.

It was a large, gloomy space – part freaky Egyptian tomb, part high-tech control centre. Big candles in ornate holders gave

the room a spooky light. Strange
maps, charts and triangular
TV screens all but covered
the blue-and-gold walls.
Large jars with lids shaped
like animal heads stood in
alcoves.

Scattered
over a Sphinx-shaped sofa
were pieces of parchment, each
marked with untidy squiggles.
Niall looked at one more
closely:

SPECIAL INVESTIGATION BY S.A.M. 117

SUBJECT: AZMAL SEKRA

OCCUPATION: SORCERER

(HATED BE HIS VILE PROFESSION!)

CRIMES: CREATING EVIL CULT OF MAGICIANS AND

PLANNING OVERTHROW OF MIGHTY PHARAOH.

WISHING TO MAKE SLAVES OF ALL HUMAN BEINGS.

LITTERING

(DESPISED BE HIS CAREFREE TRASH TOSS!).

FIRST SIGHTING OF SUBJECT: PYRAMIDS AT GIZA,

1 MAY 114 BC (EARTH CALENDAR).

LAST RELIABLE SIGHTING OF SUBJECT: RUINED TEMPLE AT

THEBES, 2 MARCH 201 AD (EARTH CALENDAR).

SUSPECTED SIGHTING: LAST WEDNESDAY

(FOLLOWED MAGICAL TRAIL).

NOTE: WAS THAT HIM OUT WALKING IN SMALL

ENGLISH TOWN? MIGHT HAVE BEEN AN OLD LADY IN

FUNNY HAT~ CHECK.

NOTE ON NOTE: IF OLD LADY, DO NOT ARREST.

UNLESS REALLY HORRID OLD LADY PLANNING TO

TAKE OVER WORLD

(LOATHED BE HER MAD DESIRE FOR

POWER!)

OBSERVATION DIARY

DAY 6

10.04

CHECKING HOUSE OF SUSPECT FOR

SIGNS OF MOVEMENT.

11.16

STILL WATCHING HOUSE OF SUSPECT. NO SIGN OF

MOVEMENT.

13.43

NO SIGN OF MOVEMENT.

15.32

AHA — I KNOW WHY THERE IS NO SIGN OF

MOVEMENT — HOUSES CANNOT BE MOVING! NOTE

TO MYSELF — LOOK THROUGH WINDOWS FOR

MOVEMENT INSIDE THE HOUSE.

16.49

HOLD ON — THIS IS WRONG ADDRESS! I SHOULD BE

DOWN THE ROAD . . .

Dark magic? Sorcerers? Cults? Niall dropped the old, yellowed paper. *What am I doing here?* he thought, suddenly scared. *Something* super-*weird is going on . . .*

With a start, he heard a muffled voice which seemed to be coming from a corner of the room. He turned and saw a tall golden casket that was shaped like a giant man, its big, blank face fringed by a headdress.

 33

Niall recognized it from spooky films and cartoons and work at school. He knew it was a *sarcophagus*, a kind of Ancient Egyptian coffin. And what did the Ancient Egyptians do to dead bodies before plonking them in coffins?

They wrapped them in bandages and turned them into *mummies* . . .

He suddenly remembered the guy with the bandaged face he'd seen on the hill.

Niall swallowed hard. As well as the voice, faint light was spilling from behind the 'door', which was slightly ajar. Who – or what – was inside?

He crept closer, took a deep breath, gripped the lid of the spooky gold casket . . . and threw it open.

There was a waft of cold air and a glare of light. Niall quickly noticed two things.

Firstly, the spooky casket was actually just a funny-shaped fridge, filled with food and drink.

And secondly, a skinny white cat was sitting on the middle shelf. Its body was half wrapped in golden bandages. A tiara sat wonkily on its head, and a dead fish was sticking out of its mouth.

Niall stared at the cat in surprise. The cat

 35

stared back at him. (The fish stared nowhere in particular.)

Then Niall screamed. The cat screamed too, before leaping into the air and banging its head on the shelf above, which made it yowl even louder.

In a panic, Niall slammed the door shut with a rattling crash. "*Meee*-OWWW, my head!"

The talking cat sounded outraged. "And my perfect little nose – you nearly bonked it! With a fridge door, if you please! I've *never* been treated so badly, not in three thousand years. Help! Police! FISH! *Meooouwwww!*"

Niall didn't hang around to hear any more from the crazy talking cat. He turned and fled from the pyramid, through the brambles and the long grass, up over the fence and down again – headfirst – into Dad's compost heap.

Groaning and spluttering, covered in muck, Niall charged back into his house, pelted up the stairs and hid under his bed.

And there he stayed for a very long time . . .

It was his own pong that drove Niall out of hiding in the end. He just *had* to go and shower before his nose exploded. At least he couldn't see the creepy impossible pyramid from the bathroom window.

If Mum won't believe me, I've got to tell my mates, Niall decided. *Show them what I saw.*

But . . . What if this whole thing was actually

a prank for some TV show? Mum and the Snitch must be in on it – and all his friends could be in on it too. He imagined what Jake and Bradley would say – *Haaaaa, you muppet! You totally believed that puppet cat was real!*

A knock at the front door jarred his thoughts. Glad of a distraction, Niall went downstairs, opened up . . . and gasped.

The bandaged man from the house on the hill was standing right outside!

Chapter Four

Weird Man, Impossible Boy

Niall stared in amazement.

The man was still wearing his sunhat and dark glasses, even though it was a cloudy day. Old, yellowing bandages completely covered his face (but Niall could see the shape of a strong nose and a square jaw underneath). He wore a raincoat and baggy trousers, and held a clipboard

 41

– his hands were wrapped in rags too.

"Greetings!" the bandaged man said cheerily.

"I saw you at the big house on the hill, didn't I?" said Niall.

"I am not inspecting trees," the man said quickly. "I have come to read your Peter."

Niall thought he must have

misheard. "Excuse me?"

"Your Peter with the gas."

"Our *meter*, you mean – the gas meter?"

"Yes! I would like to meter the Peter." The man paused. "It is a lovely evening for it."

"Morning," Niall corrected him.

"A fine time of day." The weirdo smiled again. "As well as wishing to Peter the meter, I am wondering if you have seen anything unusual around here, madam."

"*Madam?* I'm a boy!"

"Forgive me." The man made a note on his clipboard – not with a pen, but with a reed of

 43

some sort. "Suspect . . . is not . . . a madam."

"*Suspect?*" Niall echoed. "What do you mean, suspect? And why are you wearing so many bandages?"

"HUH?" The stranger jumped backwards and almost fell over. "You mean, you can see through my disguise? See my true appearance?" He gulped. "See . . . my PANTS?"

Niall grimaced. "Of course I can't see your pants. You've got trousers on!"

The man grew suddenly serious. "But you *have* seen the pyramid, am I right?"

"The pyramid next door?" Niall stared back

at him. "You mean . . . you can see it too?"

The stranger looked unhappy as he started making notes again. "You are an impossible boy. Quite impossible!"

"Hey, what are you writing?" Niall snatched away the paper, which was old and yellowed like the stuff in the pyramid. "*Suspicious character . . . possible wizard . . . ?*"

"Hey! How do you see these things that no other human can?" the man protested.

"Mum!" Niall shouted, suddenly afraid. "Mum, quick – come here!"

"Um, I must go," the man said hastily. "I am sure your Peter is a very good read. Byeeeeeee!"

Mum came hurrying from the kitchen. "Niall? What is it?"

Niall opened the door fully and looked outside. "That freaky guy we saw outside the old house on the hill—"

"That gardener, you mean?"

"He's not a gardener. He had bandages on his face and hands, and he knew about the pyramid. Mum, who can he be?" Niall showed

her the paper. "He was writing stuff about me."

Mum scowled. "What are those squiggles —
hieroglyphics or something?"

"You . . . you
really see them as
hieroglyphics?"
Niall was
gobsmacked.
"To me they look
like English! I can
read them . . . like I
could read the notes in
the pyramid . . ."

47

"Niall Rivers, this silly game has got to stop."
Mum turned away crossly and went back to the
garage. "It's time to grow up!"

"In trouble with Mummy again, Niall?" said
the Snitch gleefully from the stairs. "Or are you
just going crazy?"

"The whole *world's* gone crazy." Niall barged
past Ellie and ran upstairs to his room.

"Maybe you should move into your
imaginary pyramid!" she jeered after him.

Niall slammed his door and sighed. The man
with the bandages had to be playing a trick on
him. Like the talking cat, it was all a big joke. It

was the only possible explanation.

He had to start acting cool.

To keep himself busy, Niall kept his back to the bedroom window and worked all day on his Snitch Detector. Only now, Niall decided, it was a Stupid-Egyptian-Stuff Early-Warning System. When it was finished and working properly, he placed it on the windowsill outside, pointing at the impossible pyramid.

There, Niall thought. He decided to sleep fully dressed, in case any hidden cameras were pointed his way, and snuggled down in his bed. *Any more dumb tricks, I'll be ready for them. I'm not*

 49

going to think about it any longer. No way. Nuh-uh.
I'm not!

And of course, he was still thinking about it
when sleep finally came.

BUZZ! BUZZ! BUZZ!

The sound of the alarm clock made Niall
wake with a start. But it wasn't morning – it
was still dark outside.

The early-warning system was going off.

He sat up in bed, wide-eyed and worried.

Next moment, the window exploded inwards.
Niall covered his head as a dark brown beast as

big as a man burst into the room in a shower of glass and landed on his bed. Its face was long and pinched, with mean, hard little eyes and a protruding jaw.

"No way," Niall squeaked, rigid with fear. "You're a . . . BABOON?"

The creature screeched. It looked just like the little wooden figure still stuffed in his dressing-gown pocket, abandoned on the floor. Only this baboon was living, breathing, solid, hairy – and hissing in Niall's face.

It tensed and turned round, sticking its squashed-up hairless bum in Niall's face as it did so.

"Urrrph!" Niall spluttered. "Help! Mum! Mummeeeeeeeeeeee!"

"Comiiiiiiiiiing," came a familiar booming voice from outside, "to the rescue!"

The next moment, what was left of the window shattered as an even more incredible

figure crashed through it, swinging on a kind of vine like Tarzan.

Tarzan after a really, *really* bad accident.

Time seemed to slow as Niall stared in astonishment. The weird bandaged man was back. Only now his raincoat was unbuttoned, and Niall could see the glaring truth he'd not wanted to believe.

It wasn't just the stranger's face and hands that were bandaged. His whole body was covered from head to foot.

Completely covered.

And in that moment, Niall knew that it

wasn't only a mad baboon with a hairless bum he had to cope with.

Here, before him, was a real live MUMMY!

Chapter Five

The Beast and the Bandages

Niall watched, flabbergasted, as the mummy-man swung right inside the room, tried to kick the baboon, missed, and smacked into the bedroom wall with a massive *WHUMP!* He let go of his rope – which was actually an extra-long bandage – and tumbled to the floor.

"MUM!" Niall yelled again in terror.

"Where are you?"

"Down here," the figure called cheerily from the floor. "I am all right! I have just got a little carpet burn on my knee."

It was all too much for Niall. He scrambled out of bed and tried to run, but the baboon swung out an arm and sent him crashing into a table. With an excited chattering noise, the creature began to glow. It jumped off the bed, its fur sparkling with eerie light.

Great, thought Niall, dazed with fear. *A magic baboon*.

With supernatural strength the beast gripped

the wooden legs of Niall's desk, snarled at the mummy, and began to lift the whole thing into the air.

"You desire a piece of me, yes?" The mummy jumped up from the floor. "You crave a bit of bandage and wish to fight?" He grabbed Niall's wooden cupboard with two well-wrapped hands. "Well, two can play at that game!"

"What are you doing?" Niall cried.

"You have heard the saying, 'Fighting fire with fire'?" The mummy strained to shift the heavy furniture. "I am fighting desks with cupboards!"

The glowing baboon raised the desk above its

head, ready to fight. But then the mummy lost his grip on the wobbling wardrobe and it fell on top of him, trapping him inside – a perfect shelter – as the luminous baboon brought the desk smashing down with a splintering *SPLAMM!*

"Nooooo!" yelled Niall, seeing red as his bedroom was trashed before his eyes. How *dare* this crazy animal smash his stuff to bits! Were you allowed to punch baboons? Most of the time, probably not. But this wild, glowing nightmare was no ordinary monkey.

As the baboon bent over the remains of the furniture, Niall grabbed a broken table leg and

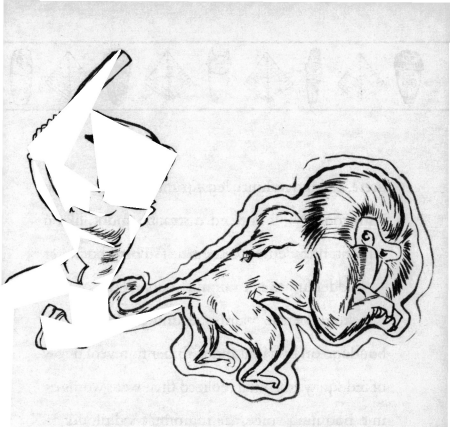

whacked the beast on its butt cheeks with all his strength.

"*GRRRR-OOOO-AAARRRRRRRR!*" The magic baboon leaped so far into the air that its head smashed through the ceiling. It dangled

there, kicking its hairy legs, grunting and snorting with rage. Niall noticed a strange mark, like a serpent, branded onto the beast's hairy back . . .

Suddenly, the mummy burst out of the wreckage of the wardrobe and peeled off the bandage on his right index finger to reveal a row of red squiggles. Niall realized they were words as, in a booming voice, the mummy read aloud:

My cause is just!
My magic is strong!
You have got on my nerves!
Now, foul beast, BEGONE!

He stabbed a bandaged finger at the baboon and, in a cloud of yellow smoke, the beast disappeared. The brand of the serpent on its back seemed to burn in the air for a few seconds; then it too was gone.

"Spell-wrap," the mummy said, fanning his face with the loose bandage. "I have got little spells like that written all over me. The trick is to find the right one at the right time. Once I was trying to banish a demon and I could only find a spell to make a bowl of pomegranate wine. Two weeks later I found the banishment spell – inside my pants! Most embarrassing . . ."

 63

Niall barely heard a word. "The baboon . . . You saved me."

"You saved me as well!" The mummy held up his hand. "Let us have a high three."

"You mean a high five?"

"No, three fingers only – the baboon is not vanquished, and may be back." He grinned. "Oh, well, whatever it was after, it failed – unless it was after a whack on the bum! You did good there, Niall Rivers."

Niall stiffened. "How'd you know my name?"

"I heard your ancestor use it at the house on the hill."

"My *ancestor*? You mean . . . my mum?"

"If you say so." The mummy clapped his hands. "Niall Rivers! Like the great River Nile in Egypt, only spelled wrongly and put in the wrong order. Truly, a great name."

"And what's your name?" Niall demanded.

"I cannot say."

"Why not?"

"Because it is a very complicated name and I have forgotten it."

"Stop acting so completely bonkers!" Niall cried. "You're no tree inspector or gas-meter reader. You were spying on that house on the hill,

 65

and you were spying on me too, weren't you? But why are you dressed up like some freaky Egyptian mummy who's had an accident in a charity shop?"

"No one has ever been able to see my true form – except you." The strange man sighed. "Well, OK. Since you ask, I am actually a two-thousand-year-old detective tracking down the enemies of my land as a Secret Agent Mummy."

Niall's voice shrank to a tiny, disbelieving croak. "Secret . . . Agent . . . *Mummy*?"

"This is so!" The stranger winked. "I am investigating some big, bad magic in your

neighbourhood right now."

Suddenly, the Snitch's sleepy voice sounded from the landing. "What's going on?"

"Hide!" Niall pushed the mummy behind the door as it creaked open.

"What . . . ?" Ellie gasped as she took in the destruction. "Oh, Niall, you've done it now!" she

said gleefully. "Mummy is going to *kill* you."

"Actually, I'm quite pleased with him," said the bandaged stranger, sticking his head out. "Greetings, small ugly child!"

The Snitch shrieked like an elephant with an exploding trunk. "*EEEEEEEEEEK!*"

At once, the mummy flicked a finger at Ellie's face. *FWAP!* A scrap of bandage slapped over her mouth, stopping the scream in a second before melting away. The Snitch went cross-eyed and

lay down on the landing carpet. Moments later, she was snoring.

"What did you do?" asked Niall shakily.

"It is called a *shaddap-wrap*," the mummy said proudly. "One of my many magical gadgets. Stops people asking awkward questions and puts them to sleep."

"Niall!" Mum screamed from the landing, her face a picture of horror and shock. "What have you—"

Quick as a flash, the mummy let rip with another

shaddap-wrap – *FWAP! SLOMP!*

"Zzzzzzzz!" In seconds, Mum was sleeping peacefully on the floor beside Ellie.

"From one mummy to another." The freaky Secret Agent beamed.

Niall looked at him. "You haven't really hurt them, have you?"

"Fear not, my young friend! They will wake come the morn, feeling most refreshed. And they will remember none of what has happened."

"Lucky them." Niall shivered in the cold breeze through the window. "You know what? I

wish I'd never set eyes on that stupid pyramid."

"It is not *just* a pyramid. It is the Pyra-Base – my portable Pyramid Base of Operations when I am on a case. It travels wherever I do, by most mystical means." The mummy raised his bandaged eyebrows. "No one is supposed to be able to see it. And yet *you* can, Niall Rivers."

"Worst luck." Niall closed his eyes. "This is just a dream. Got to be." But when he opened them again, the mummy was still there, giving him a little wave. "Secret Agent Mummy . . . bit of a mouthful. I guess that's SAM for short."

71

"Sam?" the mummy repeated. "Sam, Sam, Sam . . ." A smile spread over his face. "Sam is good. A name for me, after all these years? Yes! YES!" He started doing a funny dance with one leg in the air. "I like the sound of Sam!"

"Don't get too attached to it," said Niall. "Any second now I'm going to wake up and find you're just a figment of my imagination."

"I am not a fig of your nation," said Sam softly. "This is real. All of it."

Niall opened his eyes and gulped as he caught movement through the window. "Um . . . including *that*?"

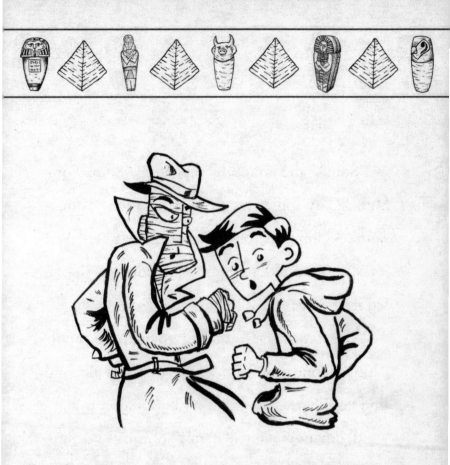

A strange dark creature with savage jaws
and shining green eyes was zooming through
the night towards them . . .

Chapter Six

A Four-Pawed Friend

Niall watched, unable to believe his eyes, as the

shadowy creature whizzed up to the

window and ...

Woofed.

He stared at the kooky,

coal-black creature floating

outside. Its head looked

metallic, with a sharp

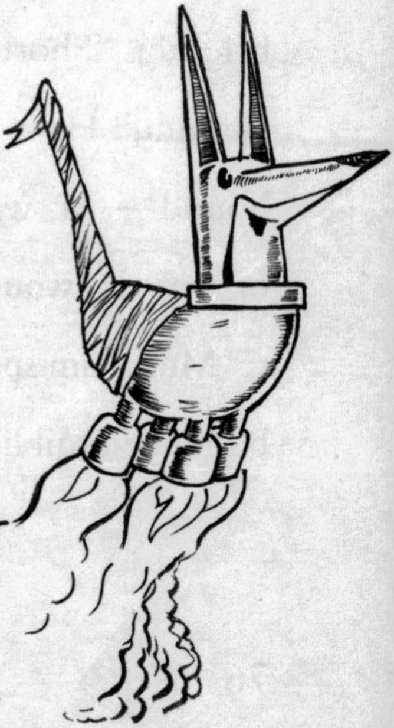

muzzle and extra-pointy ears. Jets of flame were bursting from its paws, keeping it in the air. Its rear end was wrapped in ragged bandages, right to the tip of its tail.

"It's some kind of robo-mummy dog!" Niall declared. "What a cool gadget!"

"Gadget? That is Mumbum," Sam said brightly. "Short for 'Mummy-Bummy'! He is my hunting hound — or what is left of him, anyway."

Mumbum spun his bandaged tail like a

propeller, and in a blur of light he floated into the bedroom. He dropped down onto the carpet and bounded into Sam's arms, waggling his butt madly.

"When I saw the baboon enter here, I sent Mumbum on the trail of any other magical beasts in the area," Sam explained. "Did you find any, Mumbum?"

Mumbum woofed again and shook his bottom.

Niall stared at him in wonder. "Where are you two from? Who do you work for?"

"All in good time, Niall Rivers," said Sam.

 77

"You know, long ago, Mumbum was a real hunting dog. He helped me track down many an evil criminal. But one day he met with a nasty accident." He shuddered. "Only his bum survived."

"Er . . ." Niall blinked. "How can a bum survive without a body?"

Sam smiled. "Where Mumbum and I come from, life lasts in many forms. Just look at me!"

I wish I didn't have to! thought Niall. A part of him wished he was fast asleep like Mum and the Snitch. Life had turned ᴎʍop-ǝpᴉsdn and ——

```
        p
      y   r
    a m i d -
  s h a p e d
```

Even so, while Sam might well be bonkers, he
was still Niall's best bet for getting to the bottom
of this mad mystery. And something told him
that he could trust this mysterious magical
mummy agent.

"Woof!" Mumbum barked urgently, and
started sniffing around Niall.

"He has picked up on something magical,"

Sam realized, "right here in this room! Perhaps that is why the baboon came to visit?"

With a gasp, Niall remembered the small, carved figure of the baboon-headed man in the garage. "Hang on . . ."

Sam looked confused. "Hang on to what?"

But Niall was already hurrying downstairs. He unlocked the garage door and went through. The boxes Mum had collected for Sunday's fête stood in messy stacks. Straight away he saw the crate he was looking for.

And there was the wooden statue of baboon-man – the same figure he'd seen on the pyramid

wall. The statue that had given him that strange shock . . .

"Hey!" Sam and Mumbum walked in behind him. "Nice tomb! Very dark."

"We don't keep dead bodies in here! It's for cars. And old junk." Niall showed him the strange statue. "When I touched this, just after I first met you, it sent a big jolt right through me. Could *this* be what the baboon was after?"

Sam took hold of the model.

 81

"That looks like ... a shabti!"

"Bless you," said Niall.

"No, no, I do not sneeze! I said, a *shabti*." Sam handed the figure back to Niall, looking serious. "In the old days, shabtis were models of people who could become *real* in the afterlife – to serve powerful masters. A shabti is a potent charm in my world."

"Your world?" Niall shuddered. "Yeah, well, if your world is full of magic killer monkeys, floating robot dogs and posh cats who live in fridges, I'm not sure I want anything to do with it."

Sam shook his head. "I am afraid that is no

longer possible." He pulled down a bandage on his ribcage to reveal a ruby, which he pressed. "Since we have found you in possession of a stolen magical charm, you will have to come for questioning."

"What?" cried Niall. But the ruby was glowing with a fierce red haze that soon engulfed them

both. He felt his body begin to drift. "Hey! You can't just take me away . . . !"

But a Secret Agent Mummy clearly could.

Niall felt as though he were falling through crimson custard at a million miles an hour. The baboon-headed figure seemed to buzz in his hand. Almost without thinking, he thrust it into the pocket of his hoody.

Suddenly, Niall found himself standing once again in the entrance hall of the Pyra-Base.

"You kidnapped me!" he groaned, feeling dizzy. "That's . . . well, that's . . . *kidnapping!*"

"Sorry to scare you, my young friend," said

84

Sam, shrugging off his raincoat and hanging it on the handy fig tree. "But this investigation is very important. I fear your world is in terrible danger."

"*So are you!*" came a sharp, sinister whisper from close by.

With a chill, Niall spun round. Nobody was there.

"Who said that?" Sam demanded, while Mumbum began to bark wildly. But aside from them, the room was empty.

"Help!" the mummy gasped suddenly. His top half started to shake and steam, while his

 85

bottom half seemed frozen to the spot. "So hot . . . *blazing* hot . . ."

Niall stared in alarm as the acrid smell of burning fabric filled the hall.

Secret Agent Mummy was going up in smoke!

"Sam!" cried Niall. "What's happening?"

"Under attack," gasped Sam, his bandages blackening. "*Magic* attack."

"You may have stopped my furry servant," hissed the voice from nowhere as Mumbum woofed even louder. "But you cannot stop my magic."

"Leave Sam alone!" Niall shouted.

"This fool is finished," the sinister voice hissed again. "And soon the dark and deadly power I crave shall be MINE."

Suddenly, an old, gnarled hand appeared from nowhere beside Niall! He just had time

to spot a red snake
etched into the
wrinkled skin – and
then the hand closed
on Niall's sleeve and yanked
him away ….

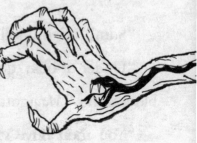

Chapter Seven

The Sign of the Crimson Serpent

"Hey!" Niall yelled as the floating hand pulled him across the sandstone floor. "Get off meeeeeeeeeeee—!"

"*WOOF!*" Mumbum flew over Niall's head with a mighty bark and caught the hand in mid-air.

89

"*OWWW!*" For a split second, the owner of the hand was visible – an old man in dark robes: his bearded face covered in tattoos. He hit the ground with a thump as Mumbum brought him down, barking furiously.

Heart racing, Niall scrambled away to where Sam was still rooted to the spot, smoking like a bonfire about to ignite.

"Right . . . hand. Biggest bandage," Sam

90

gasped. "Please, my young friend – PULL!"

Niall grabbed the sizzling fabric dangling from the mummy's outstretched hand – though it burned his fingers – and tugged hard. As he did so, a thick plug of cloth plopped out of Sam's palm and . . .

SPLOOOOSH!

Rushing water burst out with the force of a firefighter's hose. The torrent crashed into the wall like a wave against a cliff, then bounced back to drench everyone in the room!

Niall gargled as the water broke over him, and Mumbum was swept clear of the intruder by the sudden flood. But with relief, Niall saw that Sam – who'd taken the worst of the burst – was no longer on fire.

"The soaking stopped me smoking,

92

yes?" Able to move again, Sam held up the hole in his right hand and beamed at Niall. "That was my Delta Force defence – high-pressure water from the *Nile* Delta!"

"I'm just glad it worked." Niall shivered as he looked around. He glimpsed movement in the corner of the room. "Look, there's the old guy!"

Sam stared about wildly. "Where?"

"*There!* Dark robes and a red snake on his hand."

"The sign of the crimson serpent? I KNEW IT!" Sam slapped a bandaged fist into an equally bandaged palm, and winced. "Azmal

 93

Sekra, oldest wizard in the world."

Niall remembered the name from his first visit here. "You were keeping watch on that Sekra guy . . ."

"He owns the old house on the hill." Sam put his bandaged hands on his bandaged hips. "Azmal Sekra! High Priest of the Serpent Cult of Death, Doom and Disaster, you dare to enter my private Pyra-Base?"

"Where better to catch you off-guard, fool?" came the cold, mocking voice. "You bested my baboon, but you shall never defeat one as clever and evil as me!"

"We shall see." Sam peered about, and Mumbum barked in confusion. "Or we would if I actually *could* see."

Niall frowned. "How come I can see him but you can't?"

"It seems you see much that you should not," Sam answered. "Sekra is shielding himself from me."

"Yes, just as I have done for centuries!" The robed man turned and scuttled across to the fig tree. "You are so weak, mummy, you pose no threat. I can destroy you any time I choose – with any weapon." At a wave of his hand, the

fruit flew off its branches like big
green bullets.

"*WOOF!*" Mumbum
bumped into Sam and Niall,
knocking them to the floor as the
figs whizzed overhead and put dents in the wall

behind them.

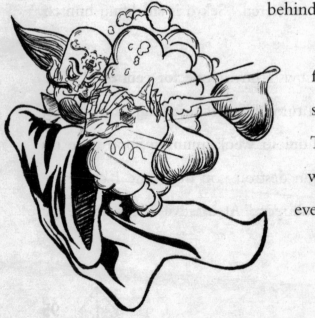

"You
filthy
sorcerer!
Those figs
were not
even ripe!"

Sam struggled up, looking all about. "Where did he go now?"

"There!" Niall could see Sekra running towards an open door at the other end of the hallway. He checked that the wooden model was still safely in his pocket. "I bet this shabti-thing got mixed up with the old junk, and he gave it away by accident."

"Well, now he has arrived in person, he shall not escape. Come!" The mummy charged off through the doorway, Mumbum barking at his heels.

Head still spinning, but not about to be left

behind, Niall sprinted after them.

He followed them through the Pyra-Base to a large kitchen with an open fire in its centre . . . up a flight of stone steps that led to a weird temple full of urns and coffins . . . through a storehouse marked OSTRICH EGGS that was full of, well, ostrich eggs, he guessed . . . into a room marked LAUNDRY, with a real, actual stream flowing through the middle, and from there through an empty CELL BLOCK with enough pyramid-shaped rooms to hold over a dozen prisoners – all of which were empty.

Emerging from the cell block, Niall burst out

of a room and almost crashed into Sam, who was catching his breath in a long, draughty corridor. Mumbum growled softly beside him.

Niall was about to ask what was up when he heard a clatter of *clip-clops* on stone.

A clatter of *clip-clops* that was growing louder . . .

Suddenly, a herd of supersized camels came stampeding into sight at the end of the corridor, heading straight for them!

"That fiend!" Sam cried. "He has let my camels out of the garage!"

Niall stared in disbelief. "You keep camels in

your garage? Why?"

The mummy shrugged. "Well, I cannot keep them in the kitchen, can I?"

Like a sandy tidal wave, they sped closer, filling the corridor as they charged, roaring like lions and baring their teeth.

"Those camels have

got the hump in more ways than one." Niall gulped. "They'll flatten us!"

"Quickly!" said Sam. "Ride Mumbum, as you would a horse."

"Ride him?" Niall echoed in alarm. "He's a dog!"

But Mumbum did not hesitate. He stood between Niall's legs and switched on his paw-jets.

WHOOSH!

Niall gasped as the robo-mummy dog whisked him high up into the air so that his hair brushed the ceiling. The camels thundered past below

him, grunting and bleating. And then the corridor was empty.

"Sam?" Niall yelled, his stomach bunched in knots. "Sam!"

"Hello, my young friend!" The ragged mummy reappeared beneath them, riding one of the wayward camels back the other way! It bleated, as if baffled by this sudden

development. "In truth, it is lucky I passed my 'Hitching a Ride on a Stampeding Camel Without Injury or Death' badge at Secret Agent Scout Camp!"

Niall grinned with relief. "I wish I knew when you were joking."

"I am most serious," said Sam. "Come to think of it, that is the only badge I *did* get." Suddenly, the camel charged off back along the corridor at a gallop. "If only I had got my 'How to *Stop* a Speeding Camel' badge . . . !"

Mumbum barked after his master urgently, but the mummy didn't hear. Niall watched in

 103

fascination as a little strip of papyrus chattered out of a slot in Mumbum's muzzle. There was writing on one side, in English – not great English, but not bad either, for a bum.

INTROODER DEETEKTED – UPSTARES

Niall held on tight as Mumbum's paw-jets burned fiercely, propelling them along the

corridor. He stopped beside a large round button set into the ceiling.

When Niall pressed it, a large stone tile slid across with a grinding noise. Tail wagging, Mumbum rose up through the hatchway into the cold darkness of the floor above.

Niall saw the moon shining in through an open window, lighting a weird throne before him. Upon it sat a scrawny little figure, watching him with glowing eyes.

Chapter Eight

Toilets, Tricks and High Explosives

Niall stared in alarm at the shadowy creature on the throne. Then Mumbum's eyes glowed like torch beams to reveal a familiar white feline, still half wrapped in golden bandages . . .

"Help! Police! Trout!" came the regal cry. "The burglar's back!"

"Oh, great," groaned Niall. "It's the talking cat."

"Miaowww *dare* you burst in here?" The feline was arching her back, tiara on her head and anger in her eyes. And now Niall saw that her throne was in fact …

"A *toilet*?" He grimaced. "What is a cat doing on a toilet?"

"Well, I'm not playing chess, am I?" The miffed moggy hopped onto the stony, pyramid-shaped cistern to reveal a cat poo in the toilet bowl. She stretched out her moth-eaten tail and flushed. But no water came out – only shiny black dung beetles. They dropped into the bowl, rolled the poo into neat little balls, and carried it away.

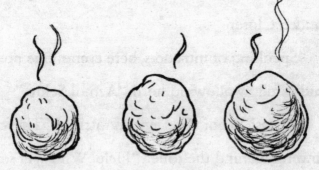

"Nice," said Niall faintly.

"It is NOT nice to have intruders when one is using the loo!" the cat said pointedly. "Nor when one is innocently eating a fish. Now, kindly get out before—"

"*WOOF!*" Mumbum barked and wriggled free of Niall's legs.

The sound of running footsteps was getting louder. Closer.

"Speaking of intruders, here comes one now," said Niall, swallowing hard. "Azmal Sekra."

"What? Who? The evil magician?" The cat cowered behind the toilet. "Help! Who will save

Great Mew, wisest and most worshipful cat goddess?

MIAOW!"

At that moment, the sinister sorcerer burst into the bathroom. Mew curled up even smaller, but Mumbum bravely flew at him like a bandaged missile.

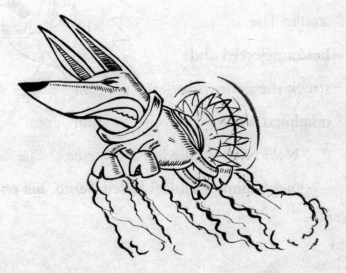

"Back, mutt!" Sekra fired a blast of dark energy from his eyes that struck the funny mummy dog with a sizzling flash.

BAM! The robotic part of Mumbum spat oil and sparks and smoke. The bottom ejected and struck the floor with a helpless whimper.

"No!" Niall shouted.

"Now, human child," hissed Sekra, his eyes

smouldering like old coals in a fire as he turned to Niall. "You have something I require . . ."

Niall backed away, terrified. Then his heart leaped at the sound of a camel approaching at high speed . . .

"Sam, quick!" he yelled. "Mumbum's blown up and Sekra's in the bathroom!"

"This is not good!" came Sam's cry outside. "Stop, my camel! Stop— *whoaaaaaa!*"

The camel stopped dead in the doorway. Sam hurtled across the room and slammed into Sekra. The old magician staggered back against the window, but quickly recovered and kicked

Sam aside. The mummy fell backwards into the loo – nearly squashing Mew – and accidentally hit the flush. In desperation, Niall scooped up the dung beetles that had tumbled back into the bowl and hurled them into Sekra's face.

"Ugh!" the magician cried as the critters caught in his wild hair and moustache. "You'll suffer for that!"

"Now, while he is busy with the beetles . . ."

Sam shook his

leg, and a small stone pyramid no bigger than a golf ball flew out of the bandages and landed at Sekra's dirty feet. "Get down! By which, I do not mean 'dance and boogie', I mean—"

KA-BOOOM!

A huge blast blew a hole in the bathroom wall, shaking the entire Pyra-Base and blinding Niall with dust. "You mean, lower your head and don't get it blown off." Reeling with shock,

he stared about as the echoes of the explosion slowly faded into the night outside. "I get it."

"*And I will get you*," came Sekra's faint and ghostly voice. "*I'll be seeing you soon . . .*"

As for the sorcerer himself – he had vanished.

"Mumbum!" Sam had seen the ragged, blackened dog's-bottom on the floor and gently scooped him up. "Oh, no! Speak to me, old friend!"

"*I'll* speak to you, you idiotic mummy!" Mew raged. "You set off a pyramid-grenade in my presence! I could have been killed! Me, Great Mew, the brains behind your whole operation,

blown up behind a toilet! Oh, the indignity!"

Sam bowed his head. "Forgive me, Great Mew."

"Don't say sorry!" Niall glared at the cat. "You and Mumbum were way greater than she was."

"How dare you!" mewed Mew, scandalized. "I am the ruling goddess of this pyramid temple. Mew the Wise! Mew the Wondrous Cat of Knowledge!"

Wondrous wind-bag, more like, thought Niall as the bandaged mutt-butt quivered feebly.

"Mumbum cannot survive for long outside

 117

his robotic dog-suit." Sam stared down miserably at the shattered metal. "Without it, he will surely die at last."

"Oh, well!" said Mew airily, licking her ruffled fur. "There's nothing anyone can do for him now."

Niall picked up the ruined dog-suit. He saw wires and metal parts poking out — and, with a thrill, found that

he understood what they did. "I'm not sure how I know this, but I think I can repair these circuits."

Mew snorted. "As if!"

"I'm pretty good with gadgets," Niall shot back. "Even freaky ones, I guess." He looked at Sam. "Do you have any tools and spare parts, that sort of stuff?"

"The Pyra-Base has a workshop," said Sam, stroking the bandaged butt as if it were a kitten. "Come. We will go there!"

Niall followed him along the corridor, and Mew trailed along behind, spluttering. "Preposterous," she snorted. "A petty human

 119

house-breaker like you, comprehending our *far* superior technology!"

"I'm not a house-breaker! But yes, somehow I think I *do* understand this crazy stuff . . . a bit, anyway." As they hurried down some steps, Niall pulled out the shabti from his pocket and waved it in Mew's startled face. "I touched this thing and it *did* something to me."

"*MEOOWWWWW!*" Mew's fur stood on end and her tiara was all aquiver. "That shabti can only have been stolen from the Temple of Thoth."

Niall blinked. "Who?"

"Thoth! The god of knowledge and secrets, worshipped by the Ancient Egyptians." As they hurried along the corridor, Mew could not take her golden eyes off the little statue. "Yes, great powers are held within, no doubt about it."

Niall shivered. "That's what Sam said."

Mew frowned. "Sam? Who is Sam?"

"Me!" the Secret Agent Mummy informed her, cradling Mumbum even closer to his chest. "Niall gave me a name. From now on, Great Mew, you can call me Sam."

"Don't think so, Secret Agent Mummy 117!" Mew retorted. "Not when I find Bandage-Pants

 121

and Dozy-Face far more appropriate!"

Niall was about to say something very rude to the cat when Sam opened a large door to reveal the workshop. It was a vast room full of palm trees planted in groups of three, with triangular workbenches suspended between them. Strange tools stuck out of the trunks, or from big clay jars.

Niall stared at a collection of mechanical Mumbum bodies on one of the tables. The heads were all different shapes and colours – a blue one with a sharp nose like a drill; a red one with extra-long ears . . .

"Once, Mumbum had many armoured forms for different tasks," Sam explained, patting the bandaged bot. "But, alas! Over the centuries they have all stopped working."

"Bummer, huh?" Niall picked up a sandstone screwdriver and got to work, fiddling about in the blue casing. "This looks less damaged than the one Sekra zapped. I think it will be quicker to fix."

Sam looked at him. "Do it, Niall Rivers, please!"

Niall got to work, twisting rusty wires into connectors and rebuilding ancient circuits.

"The shabti of Thoth has truly bestowed great powers upon you," Sam murmured. "You can see the Pyra-Base, understand the workings of our creations, detect a sorcerer who to us would be invisible . . ."

Mew was studying the shabti thoughtfully. "Thoth's seers possessed the ability to see past illusion – to unlock the truth of things and see them as they really are. For once, mummy, you are right. The boy clearly *has* been granted a certain mystical might."

BEEP! The blue suit quickly hummed with power.

 125

"Success!"
Sam carefully
placed the
bandaged
dog's-bottom
into the metal
cradle. Bolts
clicked into

place, securing him there. Then the mummy
bowed to Niall. "Bless you, my young friend –
you have saved his life."

A little piece of papyrus slid out of Mumbum's
mechanical mouth.

> FANK YOO, YUNG MARSTA.
> WUN DAY I WIL REEPAY YOO.

Niall patted the beaten-up bum and smiled. "Woof," he said.

"Rest now, my old friend," Sam murmured to Mumbum. "I swear that I will avenge the harm that has been done to you."

"But how?" Niall wondered. "This Sekra guy has some serious powers. Who is he?"

"There is much I shall have to explain to

127

you," said Mew. "But not here in this smelly old workshop! I desire and deserve more luxurious surroundings." The sniffy cat rose to her feet and tossed her head until her tiara stood up straight. "While that hopeless hound recovers, let us proceed to the operations room – where I shall expect a nice big fish, some ass's milk and a little worshipping, if you please – chop, chop!" She slunk out of the room, waving her bandaged tail. "You want answers? I'm your cat!"

Chapter Nine

Creatures of Ka-Ba

Leaving Mumbum to recover, Niall followed Sam and Mew back to the ground floor of the Pyra-Base. He jumped at every tiny noise, half expecting another attack at any moment. But other than a couple of camels standing about in one of the guest bedrooms, he saw nothing untoward.

Nothing apart from the ever-present,

 129

fruit-loops Ancient Egyptian stuff.

Why did I ever pick up that stupid carved baboon? Niall thought miserably. *Gods and monsters and magic . . . It can't be true. Can it?*

"Sam," said Niall as they walked into the operations room. "You're not a real mummy, are you?"

"I am a Secret Agent Mummy," Sam reminded him proudly.

"Yeah, but you're not, like, a dead person who's been preserved, right?" Niall persisted. "We did it at school. The word 'mummy' comes from one of the ingredients the Egyptians used

to stop dead bodies from rotting – 'mummia'. It's like tar, or something."

"Ha!" Mew curled up on the sphinx-shaped sofa. "The human mummies of which you speak are simply crude attempts to copy the *magical* mummies of *our* world."

"Right!" said Sam brightly. "Everlasting police-soldiers, like me!" He took a large tuna out of the casket fridge and began to remove the bones. "These special bandages keep me fresh. They may grow tatty on the outside, but on the inside I stay young and fit to serve my masters for evermore!"

"*What* masters?" Niall asked, a little fearful as to where his questions might take him. "I mean, where did you come from? What were you put here to do?" He glanced at Mew. "Apart from worshipping the cat and stuffing her full of fish, of course."

"Cheeky human boy!" she muttered. "You haven't heard of Thoth, but did your silly school teach you about the Sphinx, hmm? The sun god Ra? The evil god Set?"

"Er, yes. We did a whole half-term project on Ancient Egypt. It was cool."

"I fear they taught you wrongly, my friend."

Sam shook his head. "It was *hot* in Ancient Egypt, not cool."

Mew tutted. "I suppose you believe all those myths and legends to be mere made-up stories, hmm, boy? Well, in fact, they were inspired by true characters and real events in our strange and wondrous homeland – the realm of Ka-Ba."

Niall shook his head. "I've never heard of it."

"No human has. Not these days." There was a note of sadness in Sam's voice. "Ka-Ba lies in the next universe but one."

"It is home to many different powerful beings." Mew hit a button on the remote, and

 133

the triangular TV hummed into life. "Long ago, great explorers from Ka-Ba discovered a kind of tunnel through space – a gateway between the universes. They went through and came out in your world."

Niall boggled at the pin-sharp pictures on the screen. "Home movies . . . from Ancient Egypt!"

"The old Egyptians were impressed with these first visitors from Ka-Ba. They treated them like gods." Mew purred as Sam placed the fish

on a golden cushion before her. "And when others from Ka-Ba heard of this, they thought, *What fun!* and came through the gateway too. Hundreds and hundreds of them."

"So *that's* why the Ancient Egyptians had so many gods!" Niall realized. "But what about the pharaohs – the kings and queens? They were human . . . weren't they?"

"Most of them," Sam agreed.

"The pharaohs were special favourites of the creatures of Ka-Ba," Mew explained through a mouthful of fish. "They were allowed to rule in exchange for a nice bit of worship from the

 135

general public – a fine tradition that I continue here in the Pyra-Base!" She batted her long eyelashes. "I am descended directly from Bastet the cat goddess, you know."

Niall gave her a meaningful look. "I'm guessing not all of these Ka-Ba types deserved to be worshipped."

"You are correct," said Sam, pouring Mew a glass of milk. "That is why the Secret Agent Mummies were created. We guarded the pharaohs and their families! We protected their land from harmful forces! We roamed the world in pursuit of criminals and brought them back

to Ka-Ba to face justice ..."

"Let me-*owww* tell the story! I do it so much better." Mew slurped noisily at her milk, then started a slideshow on the screen. "Yes, many wicked sorts sought glory on Earth, you see. All kinds of criminals tried to hide here: demons ... cult leaders ... monsters ... dodgy bankers ... and sinister sorcerers."

Niall gulped to see the familiar face of an old man with piercing blue eyes. "Including Azmal Sekra?"

Sam nodded sourly. "Sekra was a monster. He came to Earth to raise an army of warriors

that would march on Ka-Ba."

Mew took up the story again. "He killed hundreds of humans and turned them into evil zombies under his control.

With his dark and deadly spells, he could have spread chaos and darkness across Ka-Ba and the Earth." The picture of Sekra faded, replaced by images of a squad of bandaged men and women. "Luckily, a commando force of the best and bravest Secret Agent Mummies tracked Sekra

to his secret earthly lair in Abu Simbel. There was a great battle. And though his zombies and serpent followers were slain, Sekra himself was only injured. He escaped, and swore that one day he would take vengeance on the forces of Ka-Ba."

Niall looked at Sam. "Were you at the battle?"

"Um, no," Sam admitted. "I was in bed with the mumps." He sighed. "So many of the finest Secret Agent Mummies fell that day – destroyed by dark magic."

"And so the poor old pharaohs were left with only the rubbishy junior mummies like you to

protect them. No wonder Egypt was conquered
by the Roman Empire in 30 BC!" Mew
munched thoughtfully on
her fish-head. "It was
around then that the
secret passage between
the universes began to
close . . ."

"Like a river
running dry," Sam
remembered sadly.
"The rulers of Ka-Ba
decreed that all native creatures must return

home before the link was lost and they were stranded on Earth for ever."

"But the worst criminals — like Sekra — refused to lose their freedom by returning to Ka-Ba," Mew revealed. "And since the Secret Agent Mummies were sworn to protect this world, they had to stay behind to deal with them."

Niall looked at Sam. "So you never got to go home . . ."

"No." He shook his head. "And now, I am the last mummy standing."

Mew chuckled. "You're only still around because you've been chasing these criminals for

 141

two thousand years with no success whatsoever!"

Niall didn't like the way she picked on Sam, however much of a goddess she was. "How come *you* didn't go back to Ka-Ba?"

"Um . . . er . . . *I* chose to remain on this world to feed my hunger for knowledge." Mew looked shifty. "Knowledge, yes – and FISH! Oooooooh, fish!" She rolled on her back and kicked her paws in the air. "Trout! Perch! Halibut! *Mmmmmmm-iaowwwww!* There are no fish in Ka-Ba. Not one! A terrible state of affairs, if you ask me."

"Well, anyway . . ." Niall sat down heavily on the sofa. "Thanks for the weirdest history

lesson ever, guys. But where does that leave us with scary Sekra and his killer baboon? If he's big on serpents, why has he even *got* a baboon, anyway?"

Mew coughed up a fur ball and pressed another button on the remote. "Thoth was worshipped as the god of knowledge, remember?" she began. "He was an extremely

curious fellow who looked a lot like a baboon. Naturally they became his favourite animal, so to some he granted great wisdom and eternal life – using shabtis like the one you touched."

"I absorbed a bunch of powers meant for a baboon?" Niall groaned. "Sweet!"

Mew nodded. "Thoth used these special *Ka-Ba*-boons as seers and sent them out every day to find fresh knowledge for him."

"Seers?"

"Yes, boy, *seers*!" miaowed Mew. "Oracles! Ones who could see the secrets reality tries to hide and learn all that could be learned. Many

144

were still out exploring when the portal closed."

"Like the baboon that attacked Niall tonight," said Sam gravely. "Perhaps Sekra captured it – cursed be his name! Perhaps he needed the knowledge of this baboon-seer as well as the power of the stolen shabti."

"He seems to want it back pretty badly." Niall looked at the sinister little statue. "If you need to capture him, maybe we could use this as bait to lure him into a trap?"

"Brilliant, Niall!" Sam clapped his wrapped-up hands. "But . . . where is he?"

"It's the middle of the night," Mew reminded

them, "so he is most likely at home, planning his next attack."

"The old house on the hill," Niall muttered. "And it certainly smells like a bunch of monkeys live with him."

"You should go there right now," Mew urged. "Take the fight to Sekra before he comes back here and puts my life in danger!"

"And I know just the trap we can use," said Sam. "A top-secret Secret Agent Mummy trap." He ran over to a giant urn standing in an alcove and pulled out a small black pyramid from inside. "Ta-daa! A pit-amid."

Niall was less than impressed. "A what?"

"A *pit*-amid." Sam placed it on the ground beside him. "You drop it on the floor, and when someone steps on it . . ." He plonked a bandaged foot on the device and – *FWAAK!* – a large hole opened in the ground beneath him. He fell into it. *THUNK!* "Arrrgh!" The huge urn toppled and fell into the pit on top of him – *CRASH!* "*Ooof!*" – breaking noisily as it did so.

"See?" called Sam weakly. "An instant pit, from which even magical beings cannot easily escape."

"And then you can put Sekra away for

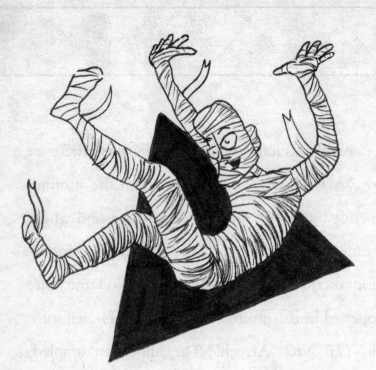

good," Mew declared. "Yes. It might just work!"

Niall's heart was beating faster. The danger he faced dated back to old Egyptian days – but now he was part of a brand-new team ready to combat it.

"Together, we might just stand a chance," he

muttered. "Watch out, Sekra – this is where *we* fight back!"

Chapter Ten

Tripping the Trap

Niall helped Sam climb out of the pit while Mew called out useless advice from the sofa. Luckily, the Secret Agent Mummy wasn't badly hurt.

"You seem a bit accident prone," Niall observed.

"That is, um, just an act to put my enemies off guard." He picked up some pit-amids and stuffed them into a large triangular bag.

 151

Then he sighed. "You know, it will not feel right, fighting without Mumbum."

Niall nodded sympathetically. "You must've fought loads of battles against evil villains together."

"Yes! Well . . . two."

"*Two?*" Niall swallowed hard. "Did you win either of them?"

"We came a good second," said Sam. "But I *did* beat that baboon in your room. I am thinking I must be on a winning streaker!"

"*Streak,*" Niall corrected.

"You want me to streak before a battle?" Sam

frowned and shook his head. "This would only waste energy. Come, let us go."

"Yes, do get on with it!" called Mew.

"Aren't you coming to help?" asked Sam.

"I must remain here to cruelly taunt Mumbum." Mew coughed. "Er, I mean, to help his recovery."

"Thank you, Great Mew." Sam bowed. "Now, Niall, are you prepared?"

"Nope," said Niall.

"Then let us go!" Sam pressed the ruby button on his ribs, and in a haze of red, he and Niall vanished . . .

 153

Niall felt the ground grow cold and solid under his feet – and gasped to find himself in the gardens outside the old house on the hill. Two rooms were lit at  the top of the house, making the windows look like eerie eyes.

"Someone's at home, anyway," he whispered.

"Let us scatter pit-amids all about," Sam said

softly, "then lure Sekra outside. He will try to get the shabti, step on a pit-amid and—"

"*Splat*," Niall concluded, pulling one of the little black gadgets out of the bag. "Sounds good. But we'd better keep our eyes peeled for serpents and baboons."

Sam winced. "I prefer my eyes unpeeled, thank you very much!"

The unlikely pair crept stealthily towards the house, then walked

backwards, spreading their little traps as they went. The trees waved their rustling branches in the night breeze, and the dark felt threatening all around.

Niall tried to keep his mind off the danger. "It's amazing to think that Ancient Egyptian stuff was copied from things in Ka–Ba. I mean, pyramids were just your houses, right? What about the Sphinx?"

"It is one of our food animals," said Sam. "Sphinx milk tastes like burnt bird nests. It is good with ostrich eggs, though."

"Nice," said Niall. "What about all that

156

Egyptian eye make-up?"

"They stole that look from rock stars on Ka-Ba," Sam explained. "And that funny dance in the sand . . ." He paused for a moment. "You know, Niall, I am very happy to have met you. You can see me, and things from my world. You gave me a name of my own. After two thousand years, it makes me feel . . . less lonely."

Suddenly, a hissing noise started up close by. An enormous, scarlet-scaled serpent was creeping towards them in the moonlit garden!

Niall froze. "I'd take being lonely any day over company like THAT!"

 157

"Sekra knows we are here," Sam realized.

"More than that, he knows the *pit-amids* are here!" Niall's heart sank as he watched

the snake slither carefully between the little black shapes. "A serpent can't step on anything."

"Oh, fang heaven's snake!" Sam pointed to another pair of crimson serpents that were winding their way towards them. "You get it, my

friend? 'For heaven's sake' sounds a bit like——"

"I get it, Sam."

"Ha! I joke to lift our spirits!"

"Please don't."

The hissing was growing louder. Sam glimpsed more wriggling shapes on the path ahead, glistening in the thin moonlight as they approached.

"Give me the shabti, Niall!" hissed Sam. "I shall use it to lead these serpents away." Fumbling for the figurine in his pocket, Niall handed it over. "Now, climb this tree. I will run and the serpents will follow. As I lure them beneath these

159

branches, drop all the pit-amids so the ground will open up around them."

"I'll try," Niall said breathlessly. Sam gave him a bandaged bunk-up and he scrambled up into the branches. "Be careful!"

Sam went racing away, the snakes slithering after him. As their hiss and wriggle grew fainter, Niall clutched the bag of pit-amids tightly, ready to act.

But he was not ready for the baboons.

With a terrifying screech they dropped down from the upper branches! The mark of the serpent was branded on their chests, and

their fangs were bared, ready
to bite.

"Get off!" Niall cried as rough hands
dragged him down to the ground. "Sam, help!"

A figure appeared in front of him. For a
second, he dared to hope it was his mummified
friend. Then he saw the aged, hideous face with

its tattoos
of coiling
serpents; the blue
eyes shining with
malevolent force.

"We meet
again, Niall
Rivers." The old
man smiled, revealing
a mouth crammed full of
broken teeth.

"Worst luck," said Niall bravely. "Look, we
know you want the shabti, but I haven't got it."

"Foolish child, it is not the shabti I seek! I have owned it already for almost two thousand years." Sekra shook his head and sneered. "No . . . I am here to take the chosen child who has *touched* that shabti and absorbed its powers. I am here for *you*, Niall Rivers. For YOU . . ."

The old sorcerer laughed and muttered a string of strange words. The very sound of them chilled Niall to the core. Suddenly, he felt terribly sleepy. *It's a spell*, he thought helplessly, his eyelids closing even as the evil magician's words scratched at his mind.

"Take him into the house, my helpless hairy

 163

slaves! Thanks to Niall Rivers, this night will be the last this world shall ever know ... the night that Azmal Sekra rules supreme over all!"

Chapter Eleven

The Temple of Sekra

When Niall woke up, he knew he was in big trouble.

For a start, he couldn't move a muscle.

He was standing statue-like in a gloomy sandstone temple. Smoke from dozens of candles prickled his nose and throat. Somewhere behind him, he could hear a clock ticking off slow, noisy seconds.

He swivelled his eyeballs this way and that, and looked all about. The high ceiling was lost in shadow. Hundreds of curling serpents had been carved into the sloping walls and the thick fluted pillars.

Niall soon saw they were not the only company he had.

The floor was patterned like a chessboard, and something stood in every square. Statues of weird creatures . . . ancient-looking contraptions . . . large stone jars daubed with enormous eyeballs . . .

And it seemed that the baboons were no

 167

longer his captors. Two with black fur stood frozen to the spot in front of him, their animal stink thickening the smoky air. To his left, he saw the brown-furred one who'd attacked his house earlier that day. Standing to his right was a fourth baboon with white fur, the familiar brand burned deep into its arm.

Niall realized he was standing in the midst of this spooky display.

And suddenly, there was Azmal Sekra beside him.

"Good. You are awake," hissed the ancient sorcerer, serpent tattoos twitching on his cheeks.

"The stars are in their proper place. The way will soon be clear."

Niall forced his lips and tongue to move. "What . . . you . . . on about?"

"Your eyes will understand what you do not," said Sekra. "For you have touched the shabti I left out for you."

"And . . . gained its . . . powers." Niall gulped. "Why . . . me?"

"Your coming was foretold long ago by Thoth's baboon seers." Sekra showed his terrible teeth in an equally terrible smile. "I have owned the shabti for almost a thousand years.

A hundred years ago, I forced the baboons to carve this splendid temple from the heart of the hillside, deep beneath the house – the house I bought two hundred years ago, knowing that one day you would live close by ... even knowing that in your twelfth year on this world, your mother would come to help with the pitiful local fête!" He sniggered. "Oh, I've had so much time to prepare for you, child ..."

Niall shivered inside. "But ... why? What ... do you want?"

"Revenge, of course. Two thousand years ago, my Serpent Cult was broken by Secret Agent

Mummies. I have killed all those left behind by Ka–Ba . . ."

"Except Sam," said Niall.

Sekra sneered. "Agent 117 was so pathetic and puny I very nearly didn't bother. But since he insisted on meddling in my plans, he had to die. I imagine that by now, he lies in pieces in the bellies of my serpents."

"No!" Niall shouted.

"Yessss," hissed Sekra. "And with the last Secret Agent Mummy dead, and with you in my grip, my vengeance will be turned against the rulers of Ka–Ba. I shall start my Cult of Death, Doom

and Disaster once more, gain new followers –
and conquer all those who oppose us!"

"But . . . there's no way to get to Ka-Ba,"
Niall remembered. "Not any more."

"Wrong!" Sekra patted the frozen, white-
haired baboon.

"Thoth's
servants
had studied
the skies, you see.
When I took control
of their minds with my
magic, I learned of a

secret *back way* between this world and Ka-Ba – a magical route that can be made to appear only when the stars and planets are in the right position . . . A route through which I could launch a surprise attack."

The four baboons closed their eyes and screeched.

"They don't look too pleased about it," Niall observed.

"I am hardly surprised." Sekra smiled again. "Their wisdom was meant for Thoth, but I forced them to give it to *me*."

"So, you've spent the last several centuries

 173

hanging with a bunch of hypnotized baboons who actually hate you?" said Niall. "Nice."

Sekra ignored him. "The beasts revealed that this back way to Ka-Ba is guarded by an invisible magical barrier. To get past it, I must perform a powerful magic ritual. And at the heart of that ritual, there must stand a chosen one who can see through magic . . . who can understand the secrets of other worlds . . . who can unlock the illusions of the universe to behold the truth within . . ."

Niall swallowed hard as everything suddenly fell into place. "Me?"

"Just as one end of the old tunnel to Ka–Ba opened by the River Nile, so Niall Rivers will open one end of the *new* tunnel." Sekra's smile had become a sneer. "So it was foretold in the ancient times. Your life has always been leading to this moment."

"But . . . why wait?" Niall was feeling way beyond scared now. "You had the shabti – why didn't you stuff the prophecy and use its power yourself?"

"That would not have been wise." Sekra tutted with fake sadness. "The ritual will join your senses to those of the mystical beings

 175

gathered around you. Your shared sight will be strong enough to see through the barriers and guide me safely to Ka-Ba ... before the powers unleashed by the portal destroy this whole pathetic world."

Niall tried to appear brave but he was terror-stricken. "You ... you can't do this!"

"Thanks to you, I can!" The sorcerer's voice began to rise in pitch and power. "I shall cross from this universe and *crush* Ka-Ba. My Serpent Cult of Death, Doom and Disaster will be INVINCIBLE! We will rule all worlds—"

"Wrong!" came a familiar voice. "You will be

locked up for ever with only your stupid snakes for company!"

Niall's eyes snapped open.

Sekra whirled round, his face twisting in rage as he saw the bandaged figure standing in the corner of the temple, dangling a bunch of limp serpents from one hand. "Secret Agent Mummy 117!"

"Sam!" Niall shouted, relief flooding through him. "You found me!"

"I was actually looking for the toilets in this place," Sam joked – at least, Niall *hoped* he was joking – and wiped his bandaged brow. "Whew! I counted five hundred steps down from that grotty old cellar. You should have a lift fitted."

"Well, well," Sekra sneered. "So you have found my secret lair at last – and it only took eighteen centuries!"

"Well, I have been pretty busy," Sam shot back, dumping the snakes on the ground. "That Pyra-Base does not clean itself, you know."

"Prattling fool!" cried Sekra. "How could you, most feeble of mummies, overcome my sinister serpents?"

"Sorry, could you repeat the question?" Sam winked at Niall. "I did not quite *catch* it!" Suddenly, the mummy flicked his wrist and sent a bandage lasso shooting out at Sekra.

179

But before the lasso could loop around the sorcerer, the white baboon bounded over to grab it and pulled hard. Sam was yanked forward into one of the spooky statues – which toppled, and thumped the baboon on the head.

"*Oo-oo-OOOH!*" the beast roared, struggling to right the statue.

Sekra clicked his fingers and the two black baboons left their squares, leaping to the attack. Sam hurled two pit-amids down in their path – but though the beasts stamped over them, no pit opened up in the floor.

"Fool!" Sekra hissed. "In the heart of the

Serpent Temple, *my* magic will defeat all others!"

"Eh? De *feet*? That is a good idea!" Sam stamped down hard on a baboon's hairy foot. The animal hissed with pain and lunged at the mummy – who leapfrogged over him and kicked the second black baboon in the stomach.

It reeled back, knocking

over one of the big stone jars.

Niall struggled to break free of the sorcerer's spell and give Sam some help. But it took all his strength just to clench his fists.

Then the brown baboon pounced and landed right in front of Sam.

Sam threw back his head and yelled at ear-

splitting volume –

"AAAAAGHHHHHH-

UGH-UGH-UGH-OOO-

UGH-OOOOOO-

UGH-UGH-

OOOOOOOOOOO-

URK-URK-URK-AAAAAAAGH!!!" He sounded like a man in desperate pain . . . or a man being desperately annoying.

"Silence!" Sekra raged. "My baboons haven't even done anything to you yet!"

"Oh." Sam gave a sheepish smile. "Sorry about that. Getting carried away." The brown baboon grabbed him tightly with both arms. "Thank you, I could use a hug."

"Sam!" Niall gasped, straining to step forward. "Got to . . . break free . . ."

The other baboons were closing in on Sam, when suddenly, the clock behind Sekra chimed

 183

like an enormous
gong. The
baboons froze.

"Cease your clowning, mummy," the
sorcerer hissed. "The hour is come. The heavens
are in alignment. The ritual must begin at
once!"

Chapter Twelve

The Power of the Portal

Sekra gestured to his beasts and they returned to their squares on the floor, the brown one still clutching Sam in its furry arms.

"There," said Sekra with satisfaction. "You will die in agony when the way to Ka-Ba is opened by your friend."

Sam looked shaken. "You . . . can reach Ka-Ba?"

"There's a special back way that Sekra needs me to open," said Niall miserably. "But if I do, the powers released will destroy the world!"

"You *shall* open it, boy. You have no choice." Sekra stalked away to the back of the temple, and bowed down to some weird Egyptian relics, muttering under his breath.

"Niall," Sam hissed. "Are you all right?"

"No!" he groaned. "But thanks for trying, Sam. How *did* you stop the snakes?"

Before Sam could reply, Sekra's voice grew louder, his chanting a tangle of hard sounds that bounced wildly around the temple walls.

186

With a chill, Niall saw that the candles were
going out, one by one. And in the
shadows that hid the ceiling from
view, pinpricks of light appeared
like stars.

The sinister
pattern of a serpent was
taking shape in the air above
him.

The
sorcerer's chant
was building to a shriek. The
serpent pattern grew brighter. It

floated down and spiralled around the frozen figures on the giant chessboard.

"Um, does anyone know the number of a good chariot service?" Sam called shakily. "I would like to order a pick-up, NOW!"

All at once, Niall heard throaty screeches in his head, and his limbs were flooded with a strange, animal strength: *The baboons' senses . . . mixing up with mine!* His view of the stars began to shift and sharpen. He almost smiled; the power was intoxicating. He was seeing beyond the serpent, his sight speeding faster and faster towards a spinning circle of eerie red light.

"There it is!" Sekra's voice was charged with excitement. "The barrier! Seek the space beyond it, Niall . . . Show me the way!"

Terrified, Niall felt a low rumbling build through the temple. The swirl above him flickered and flared.

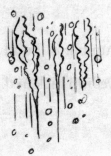

"Yes!" Sekra laughed wildly. "*The portal is starting to open!*"

The whole place was shaking. A noise like drilling grew louder in Niall's ears, and something fine and powdery fell on his face. He spluttered at the taste of it.

Rock dust?

"Wait!" Sekra thundered as the vibrations grew worse. "What is happening?"

Niall heard the fear in the sorcerer's voice. *So, this shaking isn't part of the plan?* Bewildered, he went on gazing up at the unravelling light . . .

Until the roof split open, and chunks of rubble rained down from above!

Niall yelled out as a lump of stone hit his back. It didn't just knock him to the ground – it socked him to his senses. He was finally able to move. In the gloom he saw statues toppling under a rain of rubble, baboons free too, bounding about, hooting and screeching—

And a shiny, blue-steel, bandaged dog swooping down through the collapsing roof –

a dog with searchlights for eyes and a pointed, hammering drill for a nose.

"Behold!" Sam was back at Niall's side. "Here is our chariot – right on time!"

"Mumbum," Niall cheered, "you're all right!" Tail wagging, the robo-dog swooped down and happily butted Niall's face. "Urph! Down, boy!"

"Now you know how I dealt with the snakes!" Sam beamed. "Mumbum toasted them

with his paw-jets! My loyal hunting dog couldn't bear to let us fight alone. And since you saved his life by fixing his 'Mega-Drill Three Thousand' bionic body-suit, he was able to follow us here and bring the house down on Sekra!"

"Good dog!" Niall said, petting him. Mumbum woofed happily and shook his bandaged booty like it was on fire.

But Sekra was making a less joyful racket. "Nooooo!" he shrieked, cowering beside a large coffin-like casket at the back of the temple. "Everything's out of place. The ritual is ruined!"

The temple floor bucked wildly. Niall and

193

Sam were sent staggering as an unearthly wind whipped up. The red swirl above the chessboard floor grew darker, turning and churning.

"You meddling idiots!" raged Sekra, holding his head in his wrinkled hands. "The portal to Ka-Ba was barely open when the ritual was stopped. Now it will close again – using things from here to seal the gap!"

"Um ..." Sam looked blank. "Pardon me?"

"Don't you understand?" the sorcerer bellowed. "Everything in this temple will be sucked into the void between the universes – including us!"

194

"Oh, *noooooooooo!*" Niall cried.

As the eerie gale grew stronger, Sekra scrambled to his feet and ran for the staircase. "I must get away . . ."

"Sounds like a plan to me," said Niall. "Mumbum can lift us out through the tunnel he's drilled in the hillside!"

"You go." Sam held his ground as stones and bits of statue rose up into the air and vanished in the swirling light. "I cannot let Sekra escape, whatever the cost."

But before the evil sorcerer could race up the steps, the white baboon grabbed hold of his

195

robes and tugged him to the ground.

"Release me!" cried Sekra; but the other baboons closed in and the magical gale blew even harder.

"I thought he was controlling Thoth's beasts?" Sam yelled over the hooting and howling.

"He was, for centuries," Niall called back.

"But the falling rocks knocked *me* out of my trance, so it must've done the same for the baboons." He gasped as he noticed the beasts' unmarked bodies. "Look, the serpent brands — they've gone!"

"Sekra has lost his power over his beasts. And they want revenge on *him*." As the wind gusted ever stronger and the spiral of red spun faster, Sam rushed up to the angry animals and their prisoner. "Excuse me, nice baboons!" he bellowed over the ever-building rock-rumble. "I am Sam, a Secret Agent Mummy — and you, Sekra the sorcerer, are under arrest." He looked

 197

back at Niall, grinning like crazy. "I have waited two thousand years to say that, and goodness wowzers, it felt good!"

"Noooooo!" screamed the sorcerer. "No one can stop me! NO ONE!" Wriggling out of his heavy robes, he freed himself from the baboon's grip and ran in a blind panic . . .

Straight into the tornado of fierce red light.

SLOOOOOP!

In the wink of an eye, Sekra was swept out of existence. His final screams lingered a little longer.

Then they too were gone.

Chapter Thirteen

Two Worlds

Niall stared, shaking almost as hard as the crumbling temple. "What a horrible way to go."

"Running away from baboons in just your pants," Sam agreed. "It is not good."

"I kind of meant being zapped into nothing by a supernatural storm," said Niall. "But I take your point."

"Take Mumbum's ears as well," Sam advised

 201

as the wind grew fiercer still. "I shall take his tail.
This is the moment we divide ourselves from this
place."

Niall shook his head. "You mean, it's time to
split!"

Once Sam and Niall had grabbed hold,
Mumbum activated his four
paw-jets.
WHOOOSH!
He took off
into the air,
dragging his
friends with him.

"Woo-hoo!" cheered Sam, kicking his legs as they soared up through the rocky passage Mumbum had made. The baboons used their natural agility to scramble up behind them. The supernatural storm below tried its best to suck them all back down . . .

But its best was not quite good enough.

With a mighty "*WOOF!*" Mumbum burst through a hole in the trembling dark hilltop with Sam and Niall. All three of them flopped onto the wet grass – and were almost trampled by the baboons as they tore away down the hill, clearly not about to stop for anything.

 203

"Uh-oh," said Niall: the ground around them was buckling and dipping. "I don't think the portal will settle for sucking up everything in the temple. It's going to take the whole hillside!"

"Run away!" cried Sam.

Legs aching, head still spinning, Niall sprinted after him down the rumbling slope. Mumbum followed, woofing madly. The ground made awful squelching sounds as its insides were torn

out. Niall glanced back to see the big house on the hill falling down, the debris dragged into the churning earth. By the time they reached the bottom of the hill, it was a hill no longer. The whole thing had deflated like an old balloon, leaving nothing but a patch of bubbling mud.

"It's over," Niall breathed, as monkey-hoots echoed in the distance. "What do you think the

Ka-Ba-boons will do now they're free again?"

Sam shrugged. "I expect they will continue to roam the Earth, learning all they can. One day, perhaps, great Thoth will return for them."

"Maybe he'll take you, Mew and Mumbum back to Ka-Ba too." Niall gave the mummy an encouraging smile. "Perhaps there are other, *easier* secret ways to reach your old homeland."

"I hope so." Sam patted Mumbum, who sat wagging his bandaged tail beside him. "It would be wonderful to return home."

"After all this, I think I'm ready to go home myself." Niall yawned loudly. "I'm pooped."

206

Sam frowned. "Well, it was pretty scary down there."

Niall shook his head. "No, I mean I'm really *tired*. Besides, you said Mum and Ellie would wake up in the morning. If they find me gone and my bedroom trashed, Ellie might dance about it but Mum will freak out." He shook his head. "They're not going to be the only ones, are they? A minor earthquake, a flattened hill and a disappearing house. That's going to raise a few eyebrows around the neighbourhood."

"I shall cast a know-no-magic spell over this whole area," Sam assured him. "No one will

 207

remember that there was ever a house and a hill
in the first place."

"*I* will," said Niall softly. "I still have the power
of the seer. I can feel it, like a tingle behind my
eyes."

"A thousand pardons, my young friend."
Sam bowed to him. "You are a good, brave boy,
but I know you did not ask for this magical
mayhem in your life. You must want to go back
to your safe, normal life and never see us again.
I understand. I do. I really do. Really. Yes. I do
understand. Really. I do. Yes."

"Do you?"

"No." Sam shrugged sheepishly. "In truth, I wish you would stay here in this *unsafe*, *not* normal life and see us lots! Because those other creatures of Ka-Ba who hide on Earth will have sensed the homeland magic that Sekra stirred up here tonight – and they are bound to come looking."

Niall gulped. "You mean, more freaky Ancient Egyptian bad guys will be on their way here?"

"Yes, indeed. Criminals! Monsters! Doom-mongers! Weirdos with googly eyes and pointy teeth and guns!" Sam paused. "I am not selling

 209

this very well, am I?"

"It's OK," Niall said softly. "I may not understand it all, but I'm a part of the magic of your world now. And I guess that means I can help you out from time to time."

"Oh, YES!" whooped the mummy. "After all these lonely years, Mumbum – we have a partner! We have a FRIEND!" He did a little dance, and Mumbum's tail wagged so hard that his butt nearly popped clean out of his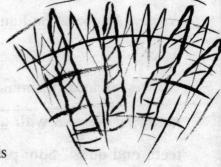

robotic body. "What a team we shall make, Niall. With your brains, Mumbum's bite and my . . . er, bandages, we can stop any bad guy, any time!"

"I have a feeling it's not going to be quite as easy as that," said Niall, but as he did so he felt a twinge of excitement. Now that he knew about Ka-Ba, his ordinary life had gone Ka-*BANG*! Who knew what mad adventures lay ahead?

Suddenly, a funny jingling of bells and drums started up somewhere inside Sam's bandaged body.

"Excuse me, that's my pharaoh-phone," he

 211

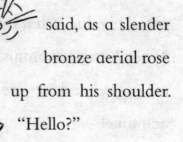said, as a slender bronze aerial rose up from his shoulder. "Hello?"

"It's Mew!" The prim, catty voice cut through the air. "It's almost five o'clock in the morning, and there's no one here to make my breakfast! Must I do everything myself?"

"Guess what, Great Mew," Sam cried. "Me and Niall and Mumbum have become a brilliant team, and we just beat Sekra! I am afraid we cannot put the vile sorcerer in the cell because

he has been sucked up into outer space in only his pants, but—"

"Yes, yes, well done, I'm sure," said the cat, yawning. "Now get yourselves back here and celebrate by cooking me some fish. MIAAOOWW!"

"You know, I think she was really impressed!" Sam smiled as his aerial retracted.

"So she should be," said Niall. "You may be the last of the Secret Agent Mummies, but today, I reckon you've come in *first*." His stomach rumbled. "And you know, I think Mew's got the right idea. I could use a little breakfast myself."

"We shall have a feast, my friend," Sam promised him. "Cheese and beef and fattened fowl, and honeyed figs and chickpeas and geese and lentils and—"

"Cornflakes," Niall suggested.

"—and cornflakes and dates and Mew's fish and ostrich eggs and lettuce ..."

"Lettuce for breakfast? Are you crazy?"

"Of course! Come. Let us hurry."

A few minutes later, Niall was riding through the sky on Mumbum's back, while Secret Agent Mummy swung from a bandage tied to the robo-dog's tail. The first rays of the rising sun lit their proud return to the Pyra-Base, with Niall's boring, ordinary house beside it. Then he groaned as he saw his smashed bedroom window, and remembered the mess inside. How could he ever explain that away?

A possessed baboon trashed my room in a fight with a magical mummy . . .

Or maybe he'd just say, "That must've been one heck of a sleepwalk," and leave it at that.

 215

It was the local fête later today. A quiet little fête on an ordinary Sunday. Niall supposed he'd have to go wandering around with Mum and the Snitch, acting like nothing had happened . . .

Mummies from Ka-Ba aren't the only ones to go flitting between two different worlds, thought Niall, as Sam looked up at him and waved. *But whatever adventures lie ahead, I'll face them at your side, Sam – my Secret Agent Mummy!*

MYSTERIES OF ANCIENT EGYPT . . .

With your wise guide and hostess – Great Mew!

Hello, lucky humans! Lucky because you're getting a second helping of MEEEEEEwww! By now you'll know that the magical realm of Ka–Ba was a big inspiration to Ancient Egypt.

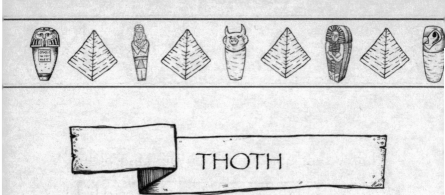

THOTH

Thoth is only one name for this god – the Egyptians called him Djehuty, but that's trickier to say! He was one of their oldest gods. Starting out as god of the moon, he soon became linked to knowledge (some believe he knew even more than me!).

In Ancient Egypt, few people could write, apart from special scribes. And lots of what scribes wrote was to do with magic. So, Thoth became associated with magic too and was trusted with many of the secrets of the gods.

I know that you have been thinking of him as a baboon but the Ancient Egyptians also liked to show him as an ibis bird.

One pharaoh thought Thoth was so important he had thirty-ton statues of him built at his place of worship in Hermopolis!

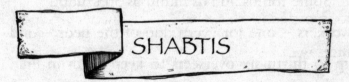

SHABTIS

Shabtis are special figurines that were used in tombs and other burials in Ancient Egypt. They were made to look like mummies with wrappings and sometimes face masks too. Their role was to

221

help the owner of the tomb by doing all his or her work! The dead, it was thought, led the same lives as they had done on Earth. Therefore they would need food and drink and slaves or helpers – and this was the role of the Shabti.

Some tombs had as many as 365 shabti workers – one for every day of the year – and up to thirty-six overseers to keep them in line! The Pharaoh Sety I was thought to have 700 shabti workers in his tomb!

We wrapped people in bandages to protect their bodies – and so did the old Egyptians, in a way . . .

THE MARVEL OF MUMMIES

Real Egyptian mummies were the bodies of people or animals, wrapped up in layers of bandages to keep them safe after death. The Egyptians believed that dead people would need their bodies in the afterlife so it was important to keep them in good condition.

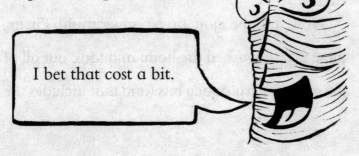

I bet that cost a bit.

Of course! So only rich Egyptians could afford it. The most expensive mummification cost one talent of silver – which today would set you back over £17,000!

To make a mummy took **seventy days**. First the dead person was taken to a priest who wore a lovely jackal mask to make him look like the god **Anubis**. Anubis was the god of mummies, and his job was to get the body ready for its journey into the next life.

Now, I hope you aren't squeamish! Firstly, these priests washed the body and took out all of the soft, slippery, gooey bits (and that includes the

brain, which came out through the nose!). Each organ was plopped into a special **canopic jar** and buried with the dead, so the body would be whole when it reached the next world.

But ONE organ was left inside the body . . .

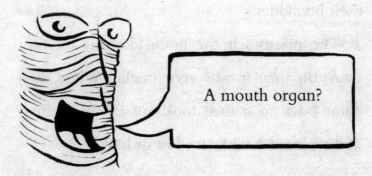

A mouth organ?

No, you idiot! The **heart**! The Egyptians thought that intelligence and emotions came from the heart, so they left it in the body.

After the priests had removed all the internal organs, the body would be left full of holes. The priests filled these holes with **stuffing**, then they covered the body in a type of **salt** to dry it out (that's why mummies look so wrinkly under their bandages!).

The priests left the body like this for fifty days. By then it was very smelly! When they came back to it they took out all the stuffing and replaced it with sawdust or linen.

Ouch! Good job these people were dead!

Yes! I never liked them very much anyway.

Next the priests wrapped the dead body in layers of linen bandages. On top of these bandages they often put a facemask and a

name label so they could remember who they had wrapped up!

Finally, if the dead person was *really* rich they would then be put into a stone coffin that the Egyptians called a **sarcophagus**.

And there you have it! The mummy was all set for its journey into the afterlife . . . But that's a story for another time. Now, who wants a fish? MIAOWWWWWW!

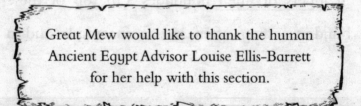

Great Mew would like to thank the human Ancient Egypt Advisor Louise Ellis-Barrett for her help with this section.

READ ALL THE
COWS IN ACTION
ADVENTURES!

JOIN THE SLIME SQUAD ON
THEIR MISSIONS . . .

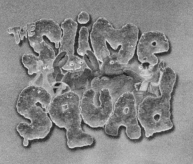

DINOSAURS... IN SPACE!

Meet Captain Teggs Stegosaur and the crew of the amazing spaceship DSS *Sauropod* as the ASTROSAURS fight evil across the galaxy!